The Test

by PJ Gray

ISBN-13: 978-1-62250-799-3
ISBN-10: 1-62250-799-1

Printed in Guangzhou, China
NOR/1113/CA21302094

18 17 16 15 14   1 2 3 4 5

Kat came home with the

test kit.

She went to her room.
She sat on the bed.
She sat for a long time.

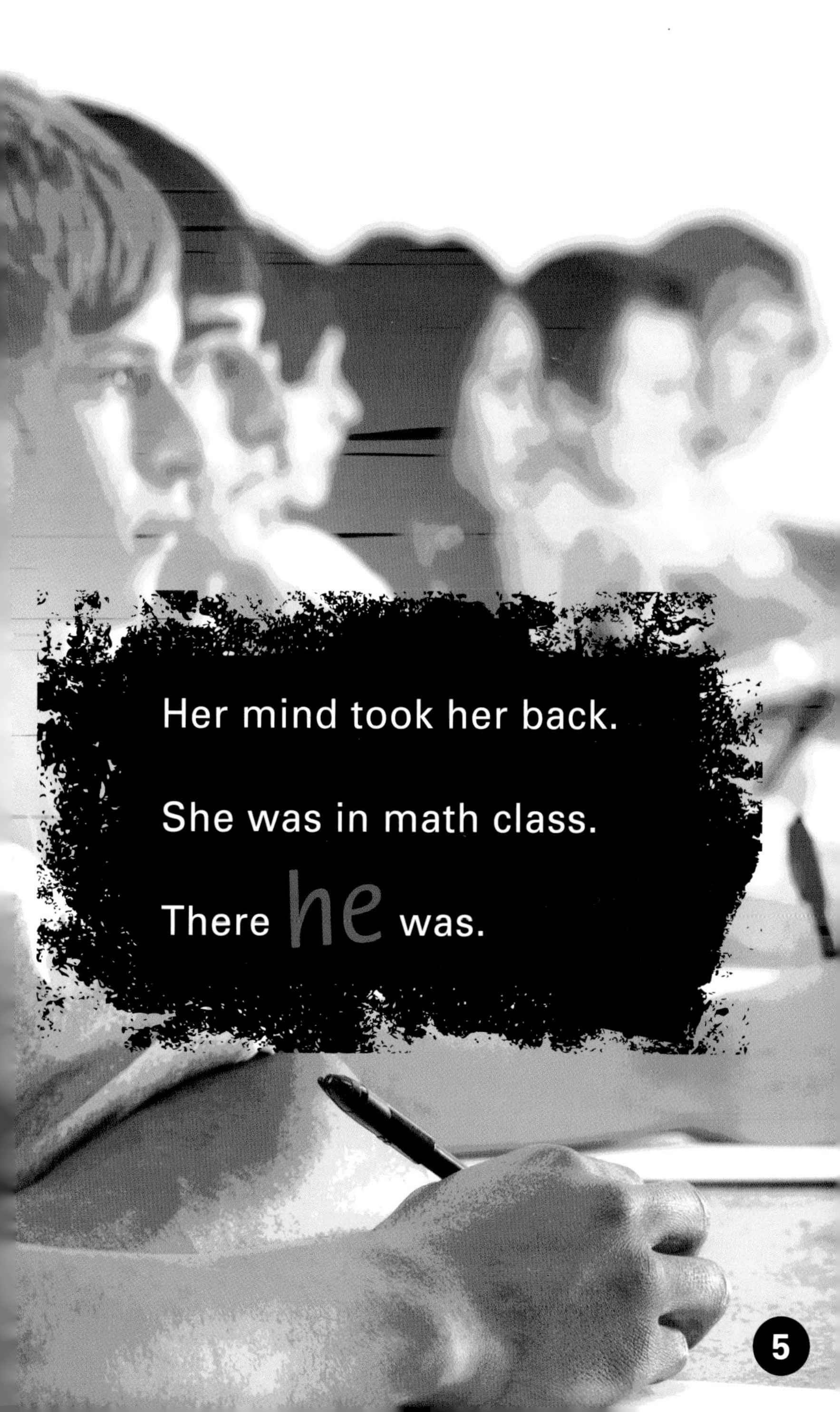

Her mind took her back.

She was in math class.

There he was.

He sat next to her.
"Hi, I'm Dan."

She saw his
smile.

His eyes were brown.

She was in love.

She sat on her bed.

The test was in her hand.

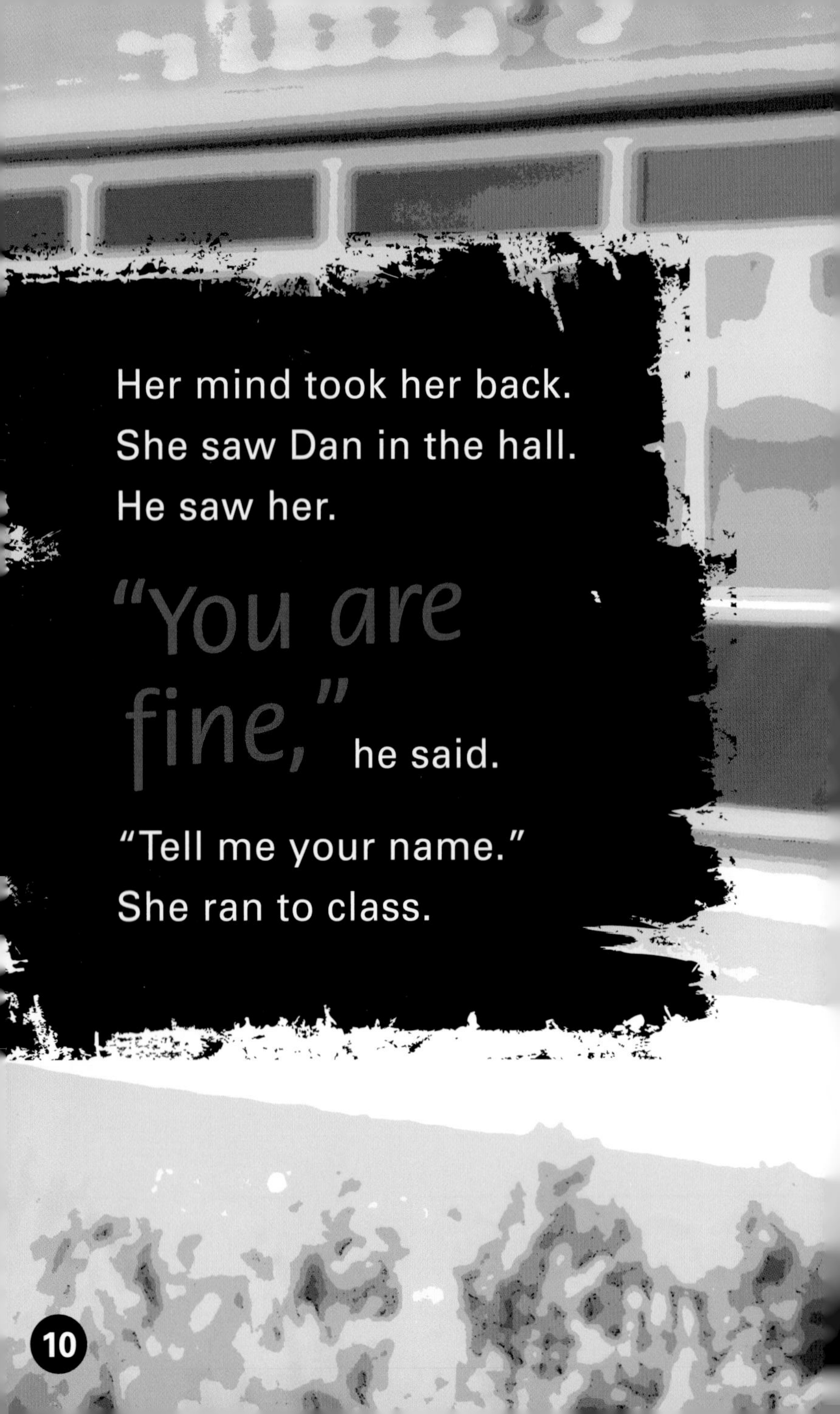

Her mind took her back.
She saw Dan in the hall.
He saw her.

"You are fine," he said.

"Tell me your name."
She ran to class.

Dan saw her at the mall.

"Tell me your name," Dan said.

"My name is Kat."

"Walk with me," Dan said.

Kat sat on her bed.
The test kit was there.

Her mom came home.
Kat sat and did not move.

Her mind took her back.

She took a walk with Dan.
"Hold my hand," Dan said.
"You are my girl."
She felt so *good* with him.

Dan had an old car.
He took Kat for a ride.
"You are so pretty," he said.
"Kiss me,"
Kat said.

Dan took Kat for car rides.
They liked to talk
and kiss.

The weeks went by fast.

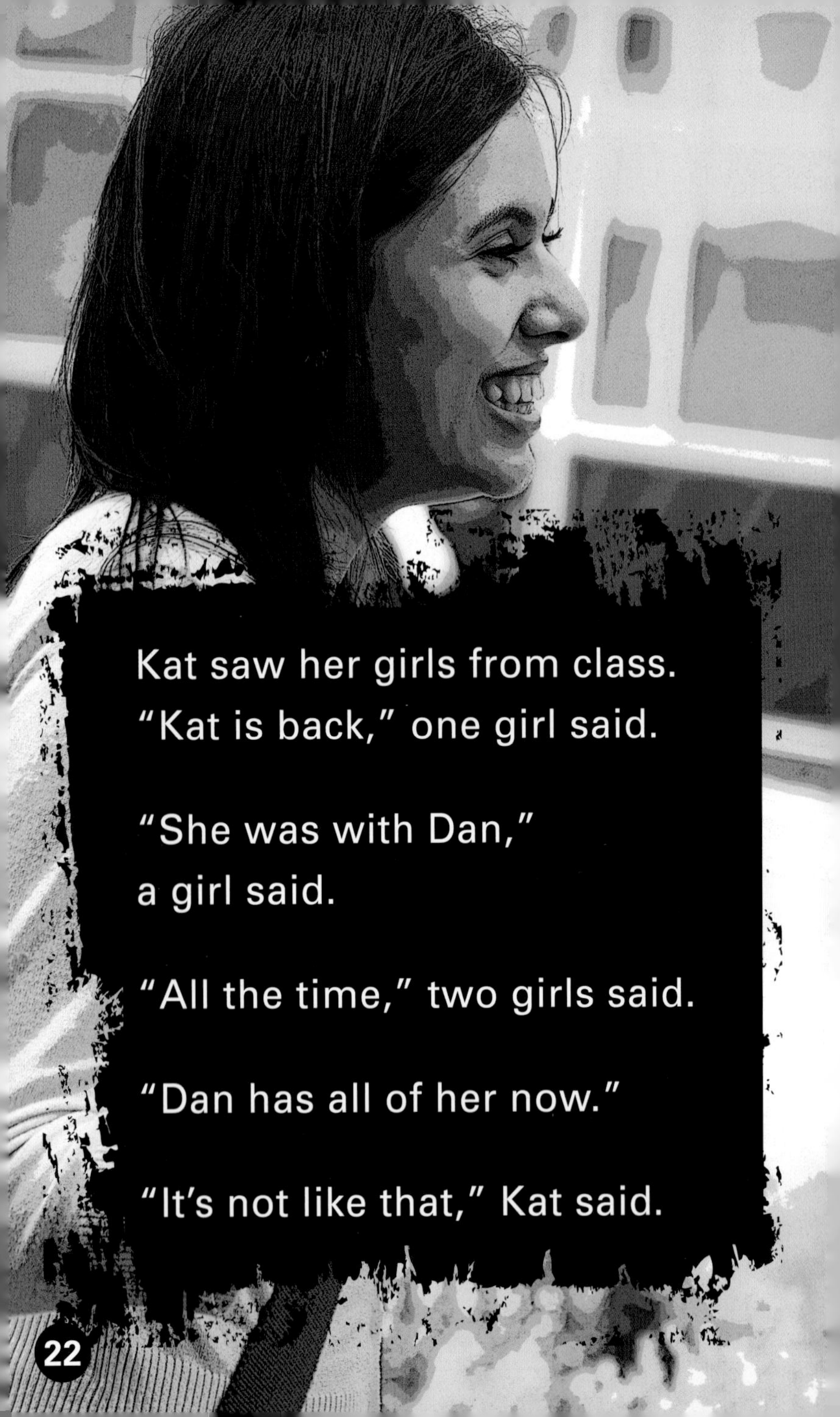

Kat saw her girls from class.
"Kat is back," one girl said.

"She was with Dan,"
a girl said.

"All the time," two girls said.

"Dan has all of her now."

"It's not like that," Kat said.

Kat sat on her bed.
Her mom was at her door.
"I am home," her mom said.

"Did you eat yet?"

"No," Kat said.

"You need to eat," her mom said.

"Not now. Please go away."

Her mind took her back.
"We have to talk," Dan said.

"Take me home now," Kat said.

"Get out
of my car!"

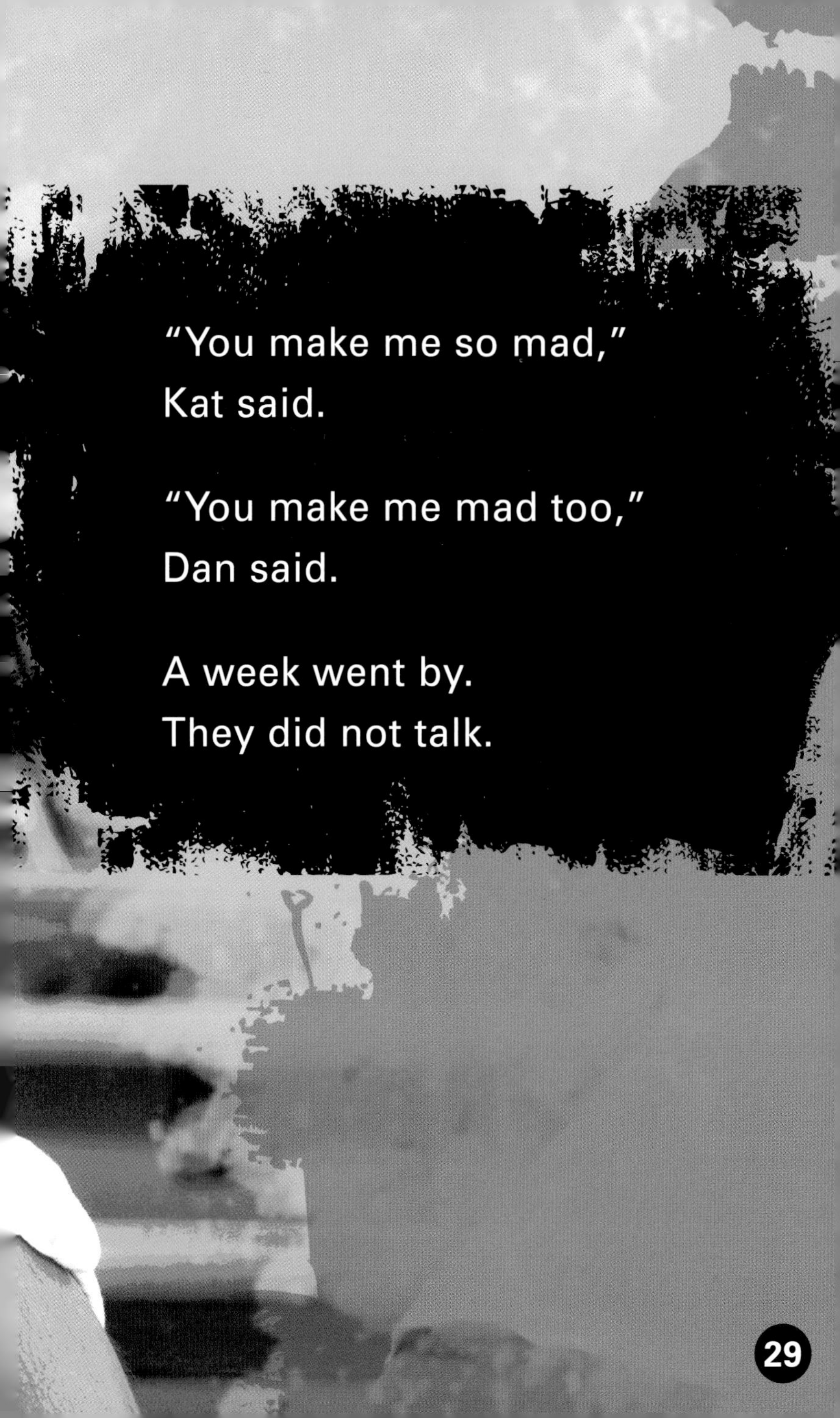

"You make me so mad,"
Kat said.

"You make me mad too,"
Dan said.

A week went by.
They did not talk.

Kat sat on her bed.
The **test** was there.

What did she want?

Her mind took her back.

She got a call.
It was Dan.

"I need to see you," he said.

"I know," Kat said.

"Can I see you?"

"Not yet," she said.
"I need a little time."

"Don't make me beg,"
Dan said. A week went by.

Kat saw Dan at the mall.
"I *miss* you, girl."

"I miss you too."
Kat got into his car.

“Take me home,” Kat said.
“My mom is not there.”
They got to her home.
Kat took his hand.
They *went* into
her home.

Kat sat on the tub.
She took
the test.
What will the test show?
Kat gave it more time.

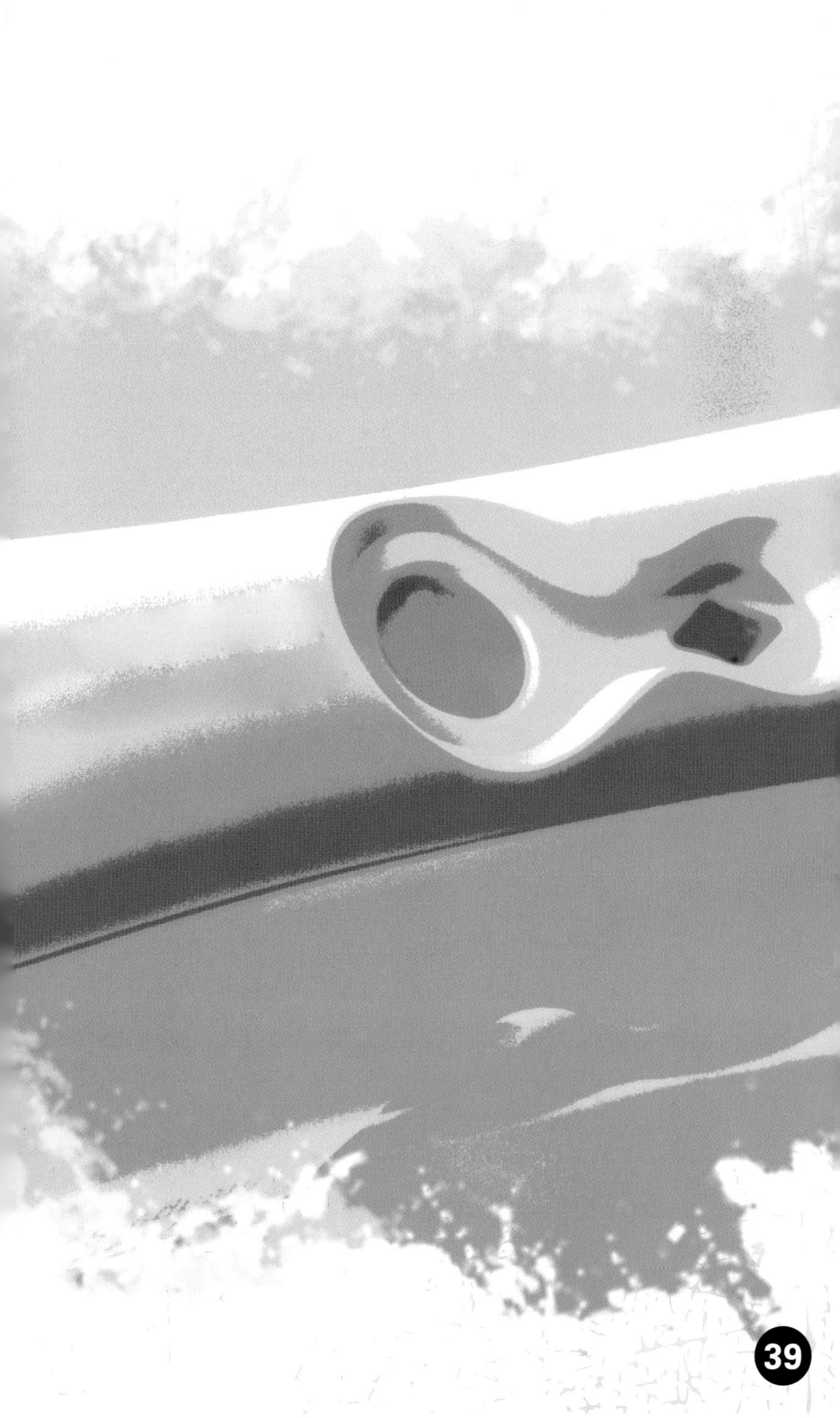

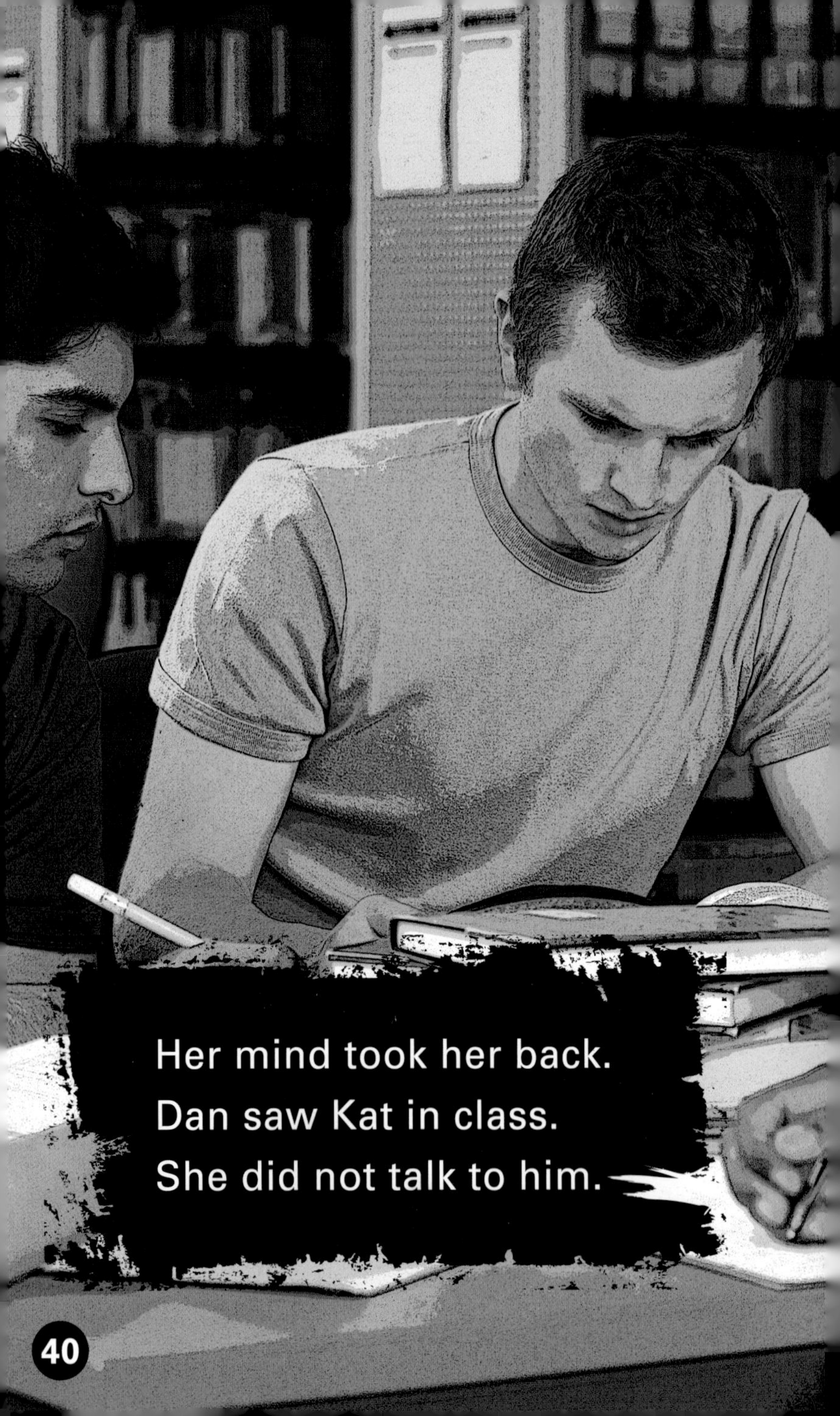

Her mind took her back.
Dan saw Kat in class.
She did not talk to him.

"Talk to me," Dan said.
"What is it?"

"I am fine."

"Tell me," Dan said.

"I told you, I am fine."

"No, you are not," Dan said.
"I can tell."

"You can tell," Kat said.
"Tell what?"

"Don't make me mad,"
Dan said.

"Don't talk to me," Kat said.

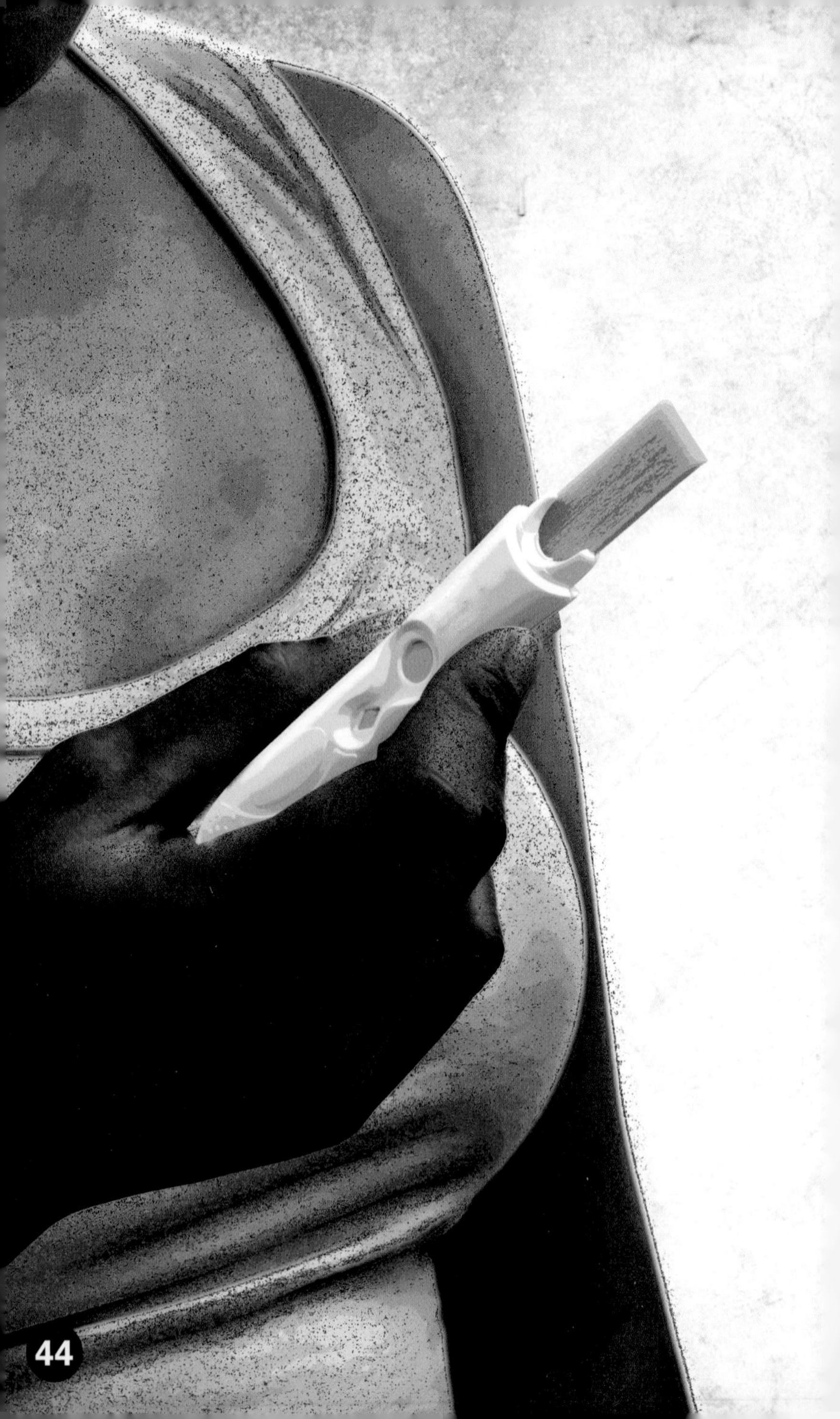

Kat sat on the tub.

She saw the test
in her hand.

She had to call Dan now.
The time had come.

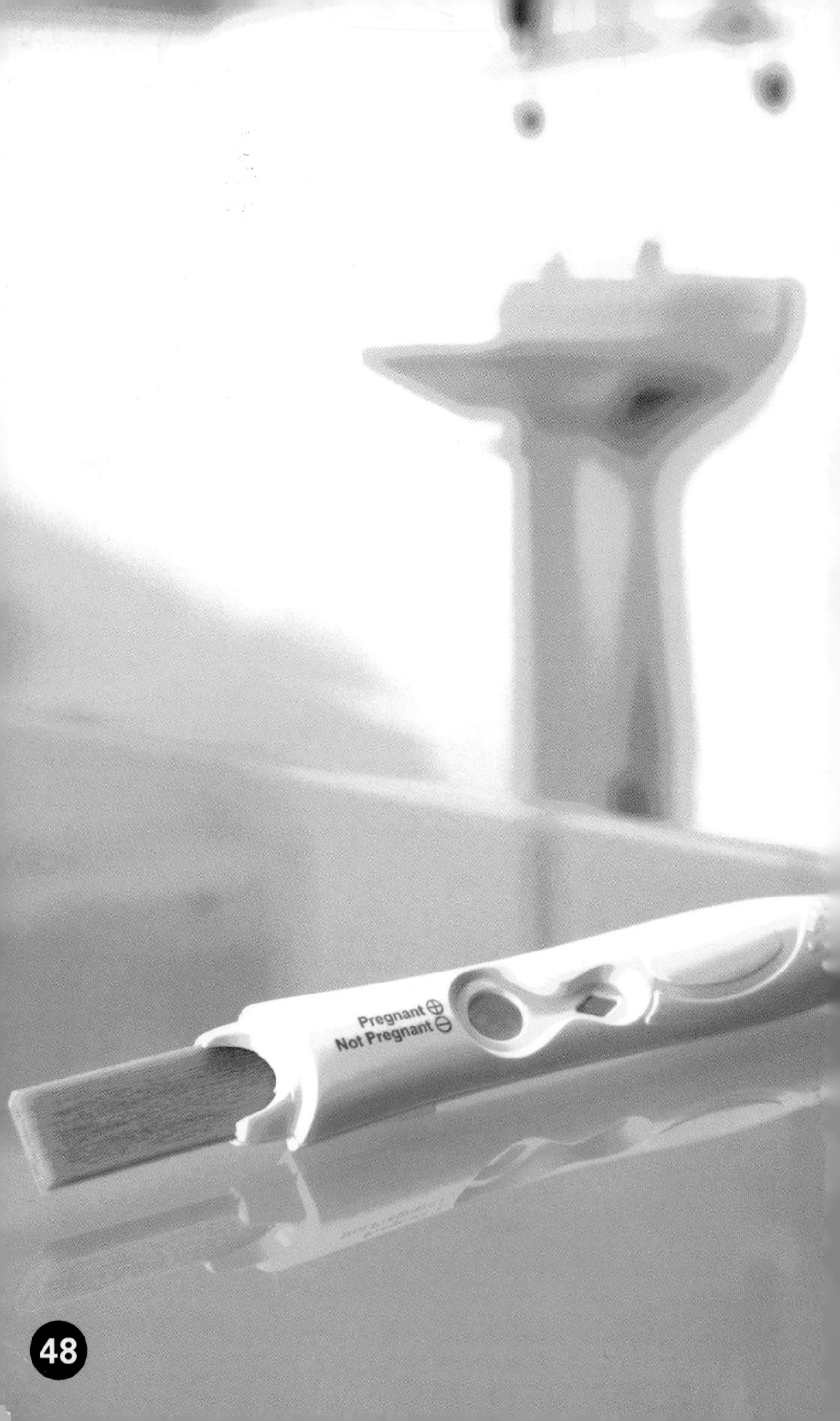
Pregnant
Not Pregnant